WITHDRAWN

Magic Squares

Learning the Inverse Relationships Between Addition and Subtraction

Colleen Adams

PowerMath™

The Rosen Publishing Group's
PowerKids Press™
New York

Published in 2006 by The Rosen Publishing Group, Inc.
29 East 21st Street, New York, NY 10010

Copyright © 2006 by The Rosen Publishing Group, Inc.

Book Design: Haley Wilson

Photo Credits: p. 9 © Burstein Collection/Corbis; p. 10 © Richard Hutchings/Corbis; p. 14 © Ewing Galloway/Index Stock.

ISBN: 1-4042-3335-0

Library of Congress Cataloging-in-Publication Data

Adams, Colleen.
Magic squares / Colleen Adams.
    p. cm. -- (Rosen Publishing Group's reading room collection. Math)
Includes index.
ISBN 1-4042-3335-0 (library binding)
1. Magic squares--Juvenile literature. 2. Arithmetic--Juvenile literature. 3. D,rer, Albrecht, 1471-1528--Juvenile literature. 4. Franklin, Benjamin, 1706-1790--Juvenile literature. I. Title. II. Series.
QA165.A33 2006
511'.64--dc22

                    2005011888

Manufactured in the United States of America

Contents

What Is a Magic Square?

A magic square is a box filled with rows and **columns** of numbers. Each number can appear only once in a magic square. When the numbers in each row and column of the square are added together, the total is the same. Adding the numbers in the 2 **diagonal** lines that cross through the center of the square also gives the same total. That is why a square like this is called magic!

The smallest magic square is a 3-by-3 square. This square has 3 rows and 3 columns of numbers and uses only the numbers 1–9.

When you add any row or column in this magic square, the total is always 15. The diagonal numbers add up to 15, too! Try it and see.

8	1	6
3	5	7
4	9	2

$8 + 1 + 6 = 15$

$3 + 5 + 7 = 15$

$4 + 9 + 2 = 15$

$8 + 3 + 4 = 15$ $1 + 5 + 9 = 15$ $6 + 7 + 2 = 15$

An Ancient Magic Square

One of the oldest magic squares is called the Lo-Shu. "Lo-Shu" means "river writing." The story of Lo-Shu is about 5,000 years old. The story tells of a terrible flood on the Lo River in China. The river god would not accept gifts the people offered him to stop the rain. One day, a turtle with a **pattern** of dots on its shell came out of the river. Each row, column, and diagonal line of dots added up to 15. The people gave 15 gifts to the river god, and the flood stopped.

The magic square on page 7 shows the pattern of numbers that appeared as dots on the turtle's shell.

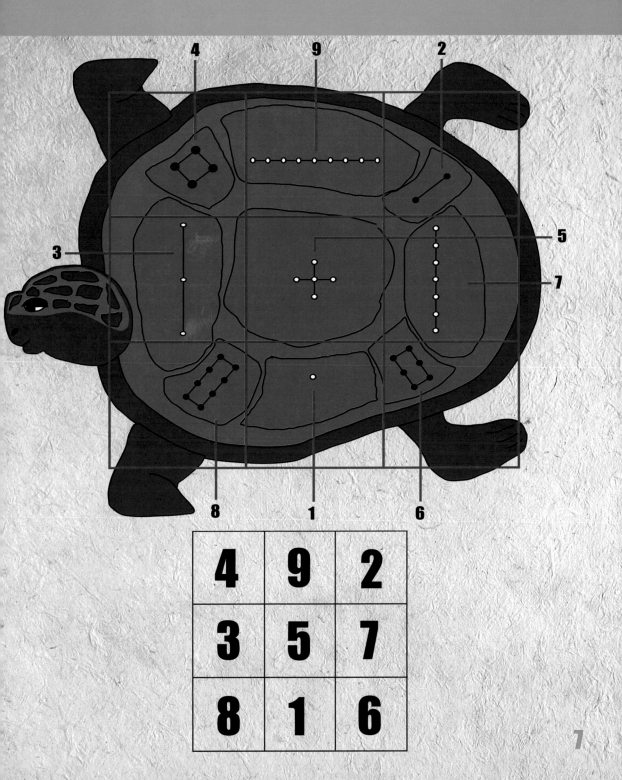

An Artist's Magic Square

In 1514, a German artist named Albrecht Dürer (AL-brekt DYUR-uhr) made a picture filled with objects that have to do with math and **measurement**, such as scales and an hourglass. In the upper right hand corner of the picture, there is a 4-by-4 magic square. This magic square uses numbers 1 through 16 and has a magic total of 34. The 2 numbers in the middle of the magic square's bottom row tell the year the picture was created: 1514.

Dürer's magic square has some extra ways to get the magic total. The 4 middle squares equal 34. If you add the 2 middle squares in the top row to the 2 middle squares in the bottom row, you get 34. The 4 corners also total 34.

Changing the Numbers Around

Learning about magic squares helps us to understand how different **combinations** of numbers can still add up to the same sum. For example, if you add 4 + 3 + 8 and then add 8 + 3 + 4, you get the same answer. Even though the order of the numbers in the second problem is **reversed** from the order in the first problem, the total is still 15. In the magic square on page 10, you can see that whether you add the numbers in a column, row, or diagonal line, the total is always 15.

If you add the numbers 4, 5, and 6 in the diagonal line that runs from the top left corner to the lower right corner, the answer is 15. It doesn't matter whether you start with the 4 or the 6; the answer is still 15. The same is true for the diagonal with the numbers 2, 5, and 8.

Subtracting Numbers in a Magic Square

We can also use a magic square to do subtraction problems. How can we take the addition we do in a magic square and change it to subtraction? Start with the total! Look at the top row of the magic square on page 13. Can you make up 2 subtraction problems by starting with the total and working in the opposite direction?

Add the numbers 4 + 3 + 8 to get a magic total of 15. Another way of combining these numbers is to add 4 + 3 = 7. Then add 7 + 8 = 15. For your first subtraction problem, start with the magic total 15 and subtract 8. Your problem will look like this: 15 − 8 = 7. For your second subtraction problem, start with the magic total 15 and subtract 7. Your problem will look like this: 15 − 7 = 8.

4	3	8
9	5	1
2	7	6

$$4 + 3 + 8 = 15$$
$$4 + 3 = 7$$
$$7 + 8 = 15$$

$4 + 3 = 7$

4	3	8
9	5	1
2	7	6

$$4 + 3 + 8 = 15$$
$$15 - 8 = 7$$

$4 + 3 = 7$

4	3	8
9	5	1
2	7	6

$$4 + 3 + 8 = 15$$
$$15 - 7 = 8$$

Benjamin Franklin's Magic Square

Many people have invented different ways of putting numbers together in magic squares. Benjamin Franklin—a famous inventor, **scientist**, and government leader—created his own magic squares over 200 years ago. One of Franklin's most popular

magic squares was made up of 8 rows and 8 columns. For this square, Franklin thought of 64 special combinations of numbers that all add up to a total of 260!

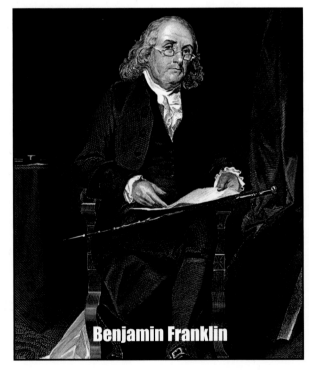

Benjamin Franklin

Glossary

column (KAH-lum) An arrangement of numbers from top to bottom.

combination (kahm-buh-NAY-shun) A group made up of two or more things.

diagonal (die-AA-guh-nuhl) Running from a top corner of a square or rectangle through the center to the bottom corner of the other side.

measurement (MEH-zuhr-muhnt) The act of measuring something.

pattern (PAA-turn) An orderly grouping of shapes or colors.

reverse (ree-VUHRS) To go in the opposite direction.

scientist (SY-uhn-tist) Someone who studies the way things act and the way things are.

Index